MW00913128

WHO SAYS SCIENCE ISN'T SCARY?

When the raccoon had finished the cat food, it walked slowly away. Two rabbits came out of the woods soon afterward, and were just starting in on the carrots when there was a crashing sound in the woods.

Something—or someone—was walking toward Bob. Something person-sized. . .

Look for these other LUNCHROOM titles:

THE FLYING POPCORN EXPERIMENT
Ann Hodgman

Illustrated by Roger Leyonmark

SPLASH™

B

A BERKLEY / SPLASH BOOK

LUNCHROOM #6, THE FLYING POPCORN
EXPERIMENT, is an original publication of The Berkley
Publishing Group. This work has never appeared before in
book form.

A Berkley Book/published by arrangement with General
Licensing Company, Inc.

PRINTING HISTORY
Berkley edition/October 1990

All rights reserved.
Copyright © 1990 by General Licensing Company, Inc.
Cover art and interior illustrations copyright © 1990 by
General Licensing Company, Inc.
This book may not be reproduced in whole or in part,
by mimeograph or any other means, without permission.
For information address: General Licensing Company,
Inc., 24 West 25th Street, New York, New York 10010.
A GLC BOOK
Splash and *Lunchroom* are trademarks of
General Licensing Company, Inc.
Cover and logo design by James A. Lebbad.
Cover art and interior illustrations by Roger Leyonmark.

ISBN: 0-425-12302-2
RL: 5.4

A BERKLEY BOOK ® TM 757,375
Berkley Books are published by The Berkley Publishing
Group, 200 Madison Avenue, New York, New York 10016.
The name "BERKLEY" and the "B" logo are trademarks
belonging to Berkley Publishing Corporation.

PRINTED IN THE UNITED STATES OF AMERICA

10 9 8 7 6 5 4 3 2 1

THE FLYING POPCORN EXPERIMENT

Chapter One

Skunks and Science

"Oh, no! There's that skunk again!"

Twelve-year-old Bob Kelly looked up, startled, from his bowl of cereal. His mother was staring out the kitchen window toward the garage. "I can't believe it's coming around here in broad daylight!" she exclaimed.

"A skunk? Let me see!" said Bob. He leaped out of his chair and rushed to his mother's side.

It was true. A plump, confident-looking skunk was trotting up the Kellys' driveway. As Bob and his mother watched, it sauntered past the garage and began sniffing the bottoms of the garbage cans.

"Hey, it's hungry!" said Bob. "Can I go out there and give it some granola or something?"

"No, Bob! Absolutely not!"

"Well, how about if I just go out there and tip over one of the garbage cans for it?" asked Bob.

"Uh-uh," said Mrs. Kelly grimly.

"What are you two staring at?" asked Bob's father as he headed into the kitchen, newspaper in hand.

"That skunk you saw the other night is back for more!" Mrs. Kelly said.

Bob's father came to stare out the window too. "It must be skunk breakfast time!" he said with a chuckle.

"At this house, at least," said Bob's mother tartly. "Bob wants to feed it."

"Feed who?" came a piercing little voice. Bob's seven-year-old sister, Lynn, raced into the kitchen.

As usual, Lynn was fully armed. She had a deep, bloodthirsty love of weapons, and she never went anywhere without at least three toy guns. That day she had a plastic sword buckled around her waist, too.

"Oh, wow! A skunk!" she shouted when she reached the window. "Don't worry, guys! I'll go trap it!" She dashed toward the back door.

"*No*, Lynn!" came her parents' voices in unison. "Don't go out there!"

Lynn halted with her hand on the doorknob. "Why not?" she asked in amazement.

"Because I'm not dealing with you getting sprayed by a skunk on a school morning, that's why not," Mrs. Kelly told her firmly.

"But I won't get sprayed!" protested Lynn. "I'll be in and out so fast that it won't have a *chance* to—"

"No way," said Mrs. Kelly. "Just sit down and eat your breakfast. You, too, Bob. Honestly, the pair of you! Let's just hope the skunk is gone by the time you have to leave for school." She walked toward the refrigerator, shaking her head.

Lynn was scowling as she dragged herself and her weapons toward the breakfast table. "The one time I get a chance to use my training, and you make me eat oatmeal instead!" she grumbled.

"What training?" scoffed Bob as he sat down again. "The Army doesn't take people until they're eighteen, Lynn. Besides, how exactly were you planning to trap a skunk with a couple of toy guns?"

Lynn glowered at him from under her eyebrows. "Is it my fault Mom and Dad don't trust me with *real* weapons?" she asked.

"Could we tone down this conversation a little?" asked Bob's father as he poured himself a cup of coffee. "Somehow I don't feel like listening to military matters while I'm having breakfast."

"Anyway, Lynn, you should leave the skunk alone," said Bob. "It's got just as much right to eat as we do. Right, Dad?"

His father stared at him over the newspaper. "I guess so," he said. "I'm not sure it has a right to help itself to *my* garbage, though."

"Why not?" asked Bob. "It's all our fault that skunks and opossums and raccoons don't have their own real food to eat. If so many people hadn't butted in here and started building houses, they wouldn't have to eat garbage! They'd be able to find grubs or worms or whatever it is that—"

"Let's not talk about grubs, either," put in Mr. Kelly hastily. "No military matters, and no grubs. Not at the breakfast table."

"Well, I know I'm right, anyway," said Bob. "If there weren't so many people around, all these animals would be able to find their own food. They have just as much right to be here as we do. Anyway, we put out birdseed, don't we? Why are birds the only animals who get to get fed?"

His mother sighed. "Everything you're saying makes complete sense, honey, but I just don't have enough sympathy for skunks, I guess, " she said. "Or for raccoons, or any other animal that tries to get into our garbage cans."

"Then why do you feed birds? Just answer me that!" said Bob.

4

"Well, because birds are—well, because they're pretty," said his mother after a second. Then, as Bob opened his mouth to protest, she added, " Okay, honey, I know that wasn't the right thing to say. I'll try to work on my attitude—but in the meantime, please finish your breakfast."

Before Bob could say any more, the doorbell rang.

"That must be Bonnie," said Mrs. Kelly with relief. Bonnie Kirk, who lived down the block, was one of Bob's best friends. She was in his sixth-grade class, and they usually walked to school together. "I guess we'll have to talk about this some other time."

Bob walked into the front hall and opened the door. "Hey, Bon," he said.

"Hi." Bonnie stepped into the front hall. "Hi, Mr. and Mrs. Kelly. Hi, Lynn. Your scabbard's coming unbuckled. Hey, have you guys heard about the ostrich that escaped from the Burford Park Zoo?"

Mr. Kelly groaned. "I thought that only happened in the movies!" he said.

"Sorry, Mr. Kelly," said Bonnie. "It really did happen. I heard about it on the radio this morning. You know those moats they have there to keep the animals on their islands? The keepers drained the one around the ostriches' area by mistake last night. One of the ostriches just walked across it and got away. So if you see him, call the zoo. They're offering a reward to anyone who finds him. His name's Ozzy, they said on the radio."

"This seems to be a big day for wildlife," said Bob's mother dryly.

"What's that person doing over there?" asked Diego Lopez at lunchtime. He was staring across the lunchroom at the vending machines.

Bob turned to look too. A trim, dark-haired woman in a suit and high heels was busily measuring the vending machines. As the boys watched, she carried her tape measure and a notebook over to the lunchroom's ornamental waterfall and gingerly stretched the tape measure across its base. Droplets of water misted her hair and shoulders, and she kept trying to shake them away. She checked the tape measure, then picked up the notebook and jotted something down in it. Closing the book, she walked toward Mr. Haypence, who was standing behind a microphone on the stage.

Mr. Haypence was the principal of Hollis Elementary School. One of his proudest accomplishments was the new, gleaming, up-to-the-minute lunchroom Bob, Bonnie, Diego, and all the rest of their friends were eating in right then. Not only had he helped draw up the plans for it and pick out the equipment and tables and chairs, but he had pestered the workers about once a minute while they were working on it over the summer. Bob's parents had told him about it after they'd gotten back from a school board meeting at which the board's president had lectured a meek Mr. Haypence. With the school year underway, Mr. Haypence liked to drop in unexpectedly at lunchtime. It was his way of making sure that no one was destroying his precious property by blowing straw papers around or letting lunch trays pile up.

He smiled at the dark-haired woman as she mounted the steps to the stage at the far end of the lunchroom.

"Uh-oh," groaned Bob. "Five hours' worth of announcements coming up. Are we in trouble for anything?"

"Not that I can remember," said Diego. "Maybe that woman's a new teacher or something."

"Or maybe he's announcing that he's engaged to her!" said Jennifer Stevens. "*That* would be worth listening to, for a change."

Jennifer was the prettiest girl in the sixth grade. She thought about only three things: herself, romance, and herself finding a romance. She was always trying to come up with schemes to work more dances into the sixth-grade schedule.

Tiffany Root, who was sitting next to Jennifer, suddenly looked worried. (That happened to Tiffany about fifty times a day, so her classmates never paid much attention. They figured she probably looked worried in her sleep, too.) "I think Mr. Haypence has a wife already!" she said. "What if he's forgotten about her? That would be a horrible mess! Do you think one of us should go up there and remind him that he's already married?"

"Great idea, Tiff!" said Bob. "I think you're just the one to do it, too. Go on up there!"

Before Tiffany could answer, Mr. Haypence started to clear his throat loudly, as he always seemed to do when he was near a microphone. Then he said, "Your attention, please! Please give me your attention!"

"Why does he always have to talk when I'm eating?" grumbled Rocky Latizano, who also was sitting at Bob's table. "He makes me lose my appetite!"

"Nothing could do that, Rocky," said Bob. "Anyway, you're always eating. If he waited for you to stop, he'd never get a chance to talk."

"Hey, I've got a high metabolism!" protested Rocky. "I'm growing very—"

He didn't get the chance to finish. "Students, I would like to speak to you about a very im-

9

portant subject," said Mr. Haypence. The woman next to him nodded emphatically and smiled again. "It's something we need more and more of in today's changing world."

"Food, I guess," said Rocky as he picked up his fifth piece of fried chicken.

"No, dances!" Jennifer Stevens's face was alight with expectation. "He's going to have another sixth-grade dance, I bet! It sure took him long enough!"

"I'm talking about science, of course," continued Mr. Haypence.

Both Rocky and Jennifer looked stricken. "Science?" moaned Jennifer. "Science is so stupid! Who cares about physics and molecules and stuff like that?"

Mr. Haypence swept on serenely. "Science! Of course, our new lunchroom is scientifically up-to-date," he said proudly. "Not every elementary school lunchroom has a walk-in microwave oven the way we do. Not every lunchroom has a waterfall. And not every lunchroom has a climate-control system as sophisticated as ours, or an automatic peanut-butter spreader."

"Which no one in this lunchroom ever uses," whispered Bob.

"But what about the rest of our school?" Mr. Haypence said. "I've been giving a lot of thought to the matter, and I've decided that we at Hollis are not doing everything we can to encourage scientific awareness. So I am naming this month Science Awareness Month."

"Well, that ought to do the trick," muttered Diego Lopez sarcastically.

The smile on the face of the woman standing next to Mr. Haypence was starting to get a little stretched. She looked as if she thought it was *her* turn to talk, but Mr. Haypence didn't seem to notice. "And at the end of Science Awareness Month, we will hold Hollis Elementary School's first-ever science fair!" he boomed triumphantly.

Now the dark-haired woman stepped up to the microphone. "That's right!" she said enthusiastically. "And I'm—"

"This is a historic moment!" Mr. Haypence interrupted her, spreading out his arms wide and nearly knocking over the woman. "For the first time, our lunchroom will house dozens and dozens of student science exhibits! Everyone is free to participate—"

Oh, good, thought Bob. *That means we don't have to do it unless we want to.*

"—except for the sixth-graders, who are required to participate," continued Mr. Haypence.

Bob slumped down in his chair.

A science fair's not a bad idea, he thought. *It's a lot better than some of the other stuff Mr. Haypence has pulled on us this year. But how am I*

11

going to come up with a decent idea by the end of the month? Every time I turn around in this place, I've got to think of a new project—or some way to get out of a new project. I'm completely idea-ed out!

Bob wasn't particularly wild about science in the first place. It wasn't that he disliked it, like Jennifer did. But every year, it seemed as though he had to learn the same stuff over again. Clouds, rocks, the circulatory system, the elements . . . it was pretty dull the third or fourth time around.

Mr. Haypence was still blaring on. "You can build wave machines. You can talk to plants and see whether they grow faster. Someone might even like to measure the effects our new lunchroom has on students' lunchtime behavior. There are hundreds of ideas to choose from! There will be prizes for the winners, and the general public will be invited to the fair. That means that visitors will have the chance to learn about science *and* to see our lunchroom!"

"Hmm," said Bob to Diego. "I wonder which matters more to him?"

Looking even more determined, the woman standing next to Mr. Haypence tried stepping up to the microphone again. All of a sudden he seemed to remember that she was there. "Oh!" he said in surprise, pulling the microphone away

12

from her. "I've been forgetting our guest! I'd like you to meet Ms. Wu. She is the school district's science-fair coordinator. It is Ms. Wu's job to organize the fair, help you with your exhibits, and publicize the event. If you have any questions, she is the one to ask."

He turned to Ms. Wu. "Do you have anything you would like to say about the science fair, Ms. Wu?"

For the third time Ms. Wu smiled and stepped up to the microphone. "I certainly do," she said brightly. "That waterfall has got to go."

Chapter Two

In Search of the Perfect Experiment

Mr. Haypence looked as though someone had just told him he had one more hour to live. He actually clutched his heart and reeled back a couple of paces.

"Get rid of the waterfall?" he gasped. "Why on earth would you want to do that?"

"We need the space, Mr. Haypence," Ms. Wu said simply. "You're going to have at least fifty or sixty exhibits in here, plus dozens of visitors walking around," Ms. Wu continued. "If you drain the waterfall, someone could set up an exhibit very nicely in that spot. The vending machines have to go, too."

"The vending machines!" Mr. Haypence practically shrieked. "Are you trying to destroy my lunchroom?"

"Oh, it's just for a couple of days!" exclaimed Ms. Wu. "The kids can handle it. Let's go for it!"

"I suppose you want us to get rid of the walk-in microwave, too!" said Mr. Haypence. "It's built into the wall. Should we just rip it out?"

For a moment Ms. Wu looked thoughtful. "There's no need for that. I suppose we could deactivate it so someone could set up an exhibit in there ... but I guess that would be a little too complicated. No, we might as well let the oven stay the way it is."

"I'm relieved to hear it," said Mr. Haypence crankily.

Ms. Wu paid no attention to his tone. She turned away from him and faced the lunchroom again. "Now, as Mr. Haypence has told you, I'm your science-fair coordinator. It's my job to see that you guys really go for it and put on the best science fair you've ever had! Of course, that won't be hard, since you've never had one before." She chuckled at her own joke. "But it's going to be a fantastic fair, I can promise you. I should know. I've done science fairs all over the county.

"Now, since the sixth-graders are all going to be participating in the fair—which I think is really great!—your teachers have agreed to let you spend the afternoon at the library—"

"Media center, you mean," interrupted Mr. Haypence.

"—at the media center doing some research. But before we head over there, do any of you have any questions?"

Diego Lopez raised his hand. "Are you a scientist yourself?" he asked.

"Well, no," said Ms. Wu. "You might call me more of a public-relations type. I'm just supposed to organize things. You guys come up with the topics. I make sure you've got space in the lunchroom, and that the fair gets space in the newspapers. But of course I'm fascinated by science," she added.

Diego didn't look too convinced. "So who judges the exhibits, then?" he asked.

"Well, there's a panel of seven judges," Ms. Wu told him. "Three of them are high-school science teachers, two are teachers from your school, I'm one—"

"And so am I, of course," said Mr. Haypence.

"That's right. Mr. Haypence wanted to be included, too." From the way Ms. Wu's tone suddenly became a little less chirpy, Bob could tell they probably had had a bit of a battle over that. "Any other questions?" she asked.

"Can we work with other people?" asked Bonnie.

"Certainly," said Ms. Wu.

Well, that's a break, anyway, thought Bob. *It might be easier to come up with an idea if I work with someone else. Maybe Diego and I can think of something together.*

"Who helps us come up with our ideas?" asked Tiffany anxiously.

"Well, I'm sure you won't need much help."

"Yes, we will!" said Tiffany tensely. "Because what if we think and think but we just can't think of anything? Or what if everyone else has used up the good ideas, and we start to lose sleep, and then we really have trouble thinking, and—"

"I'll help you if that happens, Tiffany," Bonnie said quickly from the next table.

"Thank you, dear," said Ms. Wu.

"Can my exhibit be about money?" called out Junior Smith, who never thought about anything else.

"Well, sure, if it's related to science," Ms. Wu said doubtfully after a second.

"Economics *is* a science, isn't it?" asked Junior.

"Uh, yes, I guess so. But it's not the kind of science you can do a science-fair project on. A science-fair project is more like studying nutrition in white mice."

"Nutrition! How about food? Can we do something about food?" bellowed Rocky excitedly.

17

"Or dynamite! Can we make our own dynamite?" called Louie Watson. "Dynamite is science, isn't it?"

"Or how about makeup?" asked Jennifer Stevens. "I want to create my own makeup and then do a study on how much better it makes me look!"

"These all sound like wonderful ideas," said Ms. Wu quickly. "But I think it's time to get down to the libr—the media center, so that you can start researching them! Remember, I'm going to be around for a whole month. You'll be able to bounce your ideas off me."

"Even though you're not a scientist," Diego muttered.

Bob swiveled around in his seat to stare at his friend. "Hey, what are you worried about?" he asked his friend. "You know everything there is to know about science." (That was true. Diego was a total brain.) "There's no chance you're not going to win. It's in the bag!"

Diego was frowning. "Maybe you're right. I just wish Ms. Wu seemed more like a scientist and less like a cheerleader."

"Speak for yourself," Bob told his friend. "You can have the scientists. *I* need all the cheering I can get."

Mr. Pratt, the media specialist, was a tall, gaunt man with round, wire-rimmed glasses and a face that looked like he always had a headache. He never seemed to be able to make up his mind about people coming to the media center. On one hand, he acted left out if people didn't use the center. On the other hand, he acted as if the whole room and all the media in it belonged to *him*. He never wanted anyone checking out any books, messing things up, or making any kind of noise.

He looked up and frowned faintly as the sixth graders trooped in. And when Ms. Wu had explained what they were doing there, he shook his head.

"I really don't think that's the proper way to do this," he complained. "People swarming around, getting in each other's way ... wouldn't it work better if the students came in small groups? It would be much less distracting to others, I feel."

Ms. Wu glanced around the vast, empty room. "I don't see anyone else in here right now," she said politely. "And Mr. Haypence did arrange this with the sixth-grade teachers. How about if we do a little bit of work just to get started? The kids can come back in smaller groups if they still need to."

Mr. Pratt shrugged a so-be-it shrug. "Well, if that's what Mr. Haypence wants, I guess that's what we'll have to do," he said. "All right, students. You may check the science reference section—*quietly*. And please tell me if you need any help. Don't try to do it on your own."

"Bye, kids!" called Ms. Wu in a hushed voice. "Have a great time! Go for it!" And she tiptoed out of the media center.

"Where are the makeup books?" asked Jennifer right away.

"The makeup books?" repeated Mr. Pratt.

"Well, I guess *cosmetics* is the scientific word," Jennifer said. "Where are the cosmetics books?"

"We don't have a cosmetics section," Mr. Pratt told her. "You might try the encyclopedia."

Jennifer shook her head disappointedly. "I know what encyclopedias are like," she said. "They'll just talk about makeup in Egyptian times or something. Maybe I'll try the cookbooks instead. They might have a couple of makeup recipes." She started off toward the cookbook section.

"Hey, don't hog the cookbooks!" protested Rocky. "I want to read them, too!" He barreled along after Jennifer.

Everyone was drifting toward the bookshelves except Bob. He was still standing in front of the circulation desk. "What about you, Bob?" asked Mr. Pratt. "What are you interested in?"

What *was* he interested in? All Bob could think of was the skunk he'd seen that morning.

And he had a feeling it would be too complicated to get a skunk into a science fair exhibit. "I'm not sure," he told the media specialist.

Mr. Pratt almost looks relieved, Bob thought. *He's probably glad to have one less person messing up his bookshelves.*

"Then why don't you use the card catalog and jot down a few ideas before you start?" Mr. Pratt said. "Take a good long time if you need to."

Bob walked over to the card catalog. The C drawer was right at hand level, so he opened it and began leafing through the cards.

Camels. Candles. Career, choosing a. Chemistry. Coal mining. Cocoa. Crates, how to make. Czars.

Bob quickly pushed the C drawer shut before he could faint with boredom. He was just pulling out B when he heard Mr. Pratt.

"Louie Watson! You put those back!" he hissed indignantly.

"Hey, we're using books! Isn't that what we're supposed to do?" asked Louie in a hurt voice.

Bob turned around to see what was going on. Louie and his identical twin, Larry, *were* using books—about fifty of them. The problem was that they were using them as ladders, not reading material.

"This is the only way we can reach the top shelf!" protested Larry.

"No, it *isn't*," snapped Mr. Pratt. Bob could tell he was having a hard time trying to sound mad without getting too loud. "There are perfectly good stepstools behind the counter here. All you have to do is ask for one."

"Okay," Louie sighed, "but it seems like an awful waste of time." With a tremendous thud, he jumped to the floor. Larry followed. So did both stacks of books.

Mr. Pratt winced as though someone had just hit him over the head with a hammer.

Bob turned back to the B drawer. Bananas. Battleships. Benches, how to make. (Why did Mr. Pratt think people *wanted* to make benches?) Bendy.

Bendy? thought Bob. But it just turned out to be someone's name. He sighed and resumed flipping the cards. Big Ben. Birds. Breakfast, importance of good.

I don't think I'm going to find much in the card catalog, Bob said to himself. He pushed the B drawer shut and headed over to the science section of the library.

It looked as though the rest of his classmates were coming right along with their ideas. Jennifer was using a window as a mirror and patting on some kind of invisible skin cream. Bonnie and Chantilly Lace were absorbed in a book about bees. Rocky Latizano was absent-mindedly popping Milk Duds into his mouth as he jotted down notes from something called *One Hundred Years of Ice Cream*. And Jonathan Matterhorn was staring goggle-eyed at a picture in *Your Body and You*.

Diego was sitting at a table near the reference section. He was hunched over a piece of paper and scribbling furiously.

"Hi, Diego," said Bob. "What're you working on?"

"Huh?" Diego glanced up. "Oh, hi, Bob. Nothing, really. Just some stuff about synthesizing glycoproteins."

That didn't sound like something Bob wanted to know about. "You want to work on something together?" he asked. "I'm having a little trouble coming up with an idea."

There was an uncomfortable pause.

"Uh—no, thanks, Bob," said Diego after a second. "Maybe later, okay?" Bob could tell from his tone that the two of them probably *wouldn't* end up working together.

Abruptly he turned toward the bookshelves behind him. And—as if the media center somehow wanted to come to his rescue—he saw a whole row of books that looked just like what he needed.

Edible Experiments. But Don't Touch that Socket: Experiments with Electricity. Can you be a Scientist? Money's Not Just for Spending: Experimenting with Dimes, Quarters, and Nickels. Fun with the Sun.

Okay, Bob said to himself. *There's got to be a science-fair exhibit in here somewhere. If I check out all these books, I'll find it.*

He piled up as many books as he could carry and began lumbering over to the check-out desk.

In fact, I may already have a project, he thought as he plunked down the books and saw the look of shock on Mr. Pratt's face. *I even have a title for it: "The Effect of Checking Out too Many Books on the Media Specialist."*

Chapter Three

Ideas, Anyone?

"This experiment with the quarters looks kind of interesting," Bonnie told Bob doubtfully. She held out the book she was reading so that Bob could see it. "See? It's supposed to demonstrate inertia."

"What's inertia?" asked Bob.

"It's how things that aren't moving don't want to move. And if you try to make them move, they resist."

"Oh, I get it. You mean it's how I'm feeling right now. I'm full of inertia."

Bonnie giggled. "Me, too. Except I think it's probably too many cookies, not inertia."

On the way home from school, Bob had asked

Bonnie if she wanted to do something for the science fair with him.

"Oh, I can't," said Bonnie regretfully. "I already told Tilly that I'd do an exhibit with her. We want to make our own beehive."

"With real bees?" asked Bob, startled.

"Of course with real bees! Ms. Wu has a catalog we can order them from. Anyway, I'm sorry I can't do something with you."

Even though she couldn't do a project with him, Bob was able to persuade her to come home with him and try to help him figure out what he could do for the science fair. They were sitting in the kitchen going through the piles of science books he had checked out of the media center.

Bonnie was holding out a book called *Money's not Just for Spending*.

" 'Put a stack of quarters on a tabletop,' " Bob read aloud. "Okay, I can do that." He ran up to his room and brought down the metal tackle box that held all his spare change. Quickly he fished out some quarters and stacked them up.

" 'Now, take a table knife, and' —hang on, Bon," Bob said. He got up from the table, rummaged in a drawer, and came back to where Bonnie was sitting. He spilled onto the table a handful of peanut-butter cookies he had snagged from the cupboard on the way back. "One knife," he said, and consulted the book again. "Now what do I do?"

"'Take the knife and make a quick slicing motion under the stack of quarters. One by one, the quarters will fly out of the stack. Because of inertia, the rest of the stack will remain undisturbed.'"

Bob picked up the knife, gave the stack of quarters a skeptical glance, and then quickly slid the knife under the stack. It worked! The bottom quarter slid out of the stack, skidded across the table, bounced to the floor, and rolled away under the dishwasher.

"Hey, that's great! It really works!" said Bonnie.

Bob was excited, too. "Let me try it again," he said. Once again he sliced another quarter out of the pile without any trouble. He sliced out another, and another.

Then he paused. "Okay, so it works," he said slowly. "But what am I going to *do* with it? Stand at my booth at the science fair and slice quarters out of a stack? That doesn't sound too thrilling."

Bonnie sighed. "I guess you're right," she said, picking up another book and flipping through it. "What about this experiment here?" She pointed to another picture. "You can create a siphon and show how you can make water run uphill before it goes down."

"Hmm," said Bob, glancing at the directions in the book. "Sounds okay. Let me see if we've got the stuff we need for it."

"Mom!" he shouted up the stairs with the book in his hand.

"Yes, dear?"

"Do we have a rubber or plastic tube about three feet long and not more than one-half inch in diameter, two water pails, and water?"

"What?" his mother called back. She came to the top of the stairs and peered into the kitchen. "Oh, you're reading that out of a book! Well, we've got the water and the buckets, honey, but we don't have any tubing in the house right now."

"Oh," said Bob. He and Bonnie sighed.

Once again inertia settled over the two of them.

"Now, what exactly are you two going to be doing?" Mrs. Kelly asked Bob and his father.

"Honey, don't worry," said Mr. Kelly jovially. "You'll be grateful to us when we're done with this experiment, believe me."

It was Saturday morning, a couple of days after Bob had realized that a stack of quarters wasn't much of a science fair exhibit. He had asked his father for help, but both he and his mother were beginning to wonder whether that had been a good idea.

"You know, I won a lot of prizes at science fairs when I was a kid," Mr. Kelly went on. "I'm just going to give Bob a hand."

Only it looked as if he wanted to give more than a hand. He seemed to want to give his whole body—and win first prize himself, too.

And besides that, he wanted to rewire the entire house.

"Dad, I don't quite get this idea, either, " said Bob as the three of them made their way down to the basement. "Tell me again what we're doing?"

"We're turning our house into a smart house," said Mr. Kelly excitedly.

"Oh no you're not! This house is already as smart as it needs to be," said Mrs. Kelly.

Bob's father just brushed that aside. "You won't think that when Bob and I are done. We're going to build a control panel down here that will operate every room on a timer system."

"Operate every room? How do you mean?" asked Bob.

"Well, say it's time for the dishwasher to run. This panel will switch it on automatically from down here. This way, we won't have to be in the kitchen punching all those dishwasher buttons. We won't even have to be in the house!"

"But Dad, it's not that hard to start the dishwasher by hand—"

Bob's father interrupted him. "That's not the point, Bob. The point is that we're creating a very sophisticated system to make our house completely self-reliant. Don't you think that's exciting? I bet those judges will love it!"

"Um, sure, Dad. But do you know how to do all this? You're not an electrician!"

"Oh, between the two of us we can figure it out," said Mr. Kelly breezily. "Most of these appliances are pretty self-explanatory."

"I hope so," said Bob's mother as she headed up the steps. She was taking Lynn out to buy some new clothes, an ordeal for both of them. "I already know I'm going to be in a bad mood when I get home. If I come home to a house that's smarter than I am, I'm *really* going to be in a bad mood."

There wasn't much danger of her coming home to a house that was smarter than she was. Two hours later, the insides of two TVs, the VCR, the dishwasher, the microwave, the hot-air corn popper, the CD player, and the toaster oven were spread out in layers on the basement floor. And they were looking less self-explanatory by the minute.

"Hand me that wire, will you?" asked Mr. Kelly. He was kneeling over the back of the new control panel and breathing hard as he fumblingly adjusted a tiny, tiny screw with a tiny, tiny screwdriver.

Bob looked around blankly. "Which one?" he asked. There were so many wires spread out around them that he felt as though he were sitting in the middle of a spiderweb.

"*That* one! *That* one!" said his father, gesturing with the tiny screwdriver. He was starting to sound a little grumpy. "The one I'm pointing to!"

The wire Mr. Kelly was pointing to was poking out from under a big, messy pile of TV guts. Bob yanked at it, but it wouldn't come loose. Bob stood up, planning to try to get at it from the other side—and accidentally stepped right through one of the TV screens.

His father reared up from the control panel. "*Bob!*" he shouted. "What is going on here?"

"Dad, I'm sorry!" said Bob, struggling to shake the TV screen off his foot. "I couldn't help it!"

"You don't seem to be paying much attention. Don't you want me to help you with your project?" Mr. Kelly snapped.

"Yes, but I only wanted you to help me come up with an idea! I didn't want you to make me tear the whole house apart! *You're* the one who's trying to get this first prize, not me!"

There, thought Bob defiantly. *I said what I thought. Now go ahead and kill me.*

There was silence in the basement while he and his father stared at each other.

"I guess you're right," said Mr. Kelly after a second. "Sorry, Bob. I didn't mean to get carried away." He glanced ruefully at the heaps of appliance debris all around them. "And I see that I *did* get a little carried away. What time is it, anyway?"

"Two-fifteen," said Bob. His stomach started growling, right on cue.

"Let's go get some lunch," said his father. "And then we can come down and clean up all this mess. I mean, *I'll* clean it up."

He gave Bob's shoulder a pat as the two of them walked toward the cellar stairs. Then he stopped short.

"We don't have anything to make lunch with," he said. "The whole kitchen's on the floor down here."

"Attention, all students!" came Mr. Haypence's voice on the public-address system. It was Monday morning, and everyone was starting to trickle into their classrooms.

"Attention!" Mr. Haypence said again. "I would like to warn all students that the escaped ostrich has been spotted in our vicinity."

"Hey, great!" shouted about half the kids in the classrooms.

Of course, Mr. Haypence couldn't hear them. "I am told that the ostrich answers to the name

32

of Ozzy—a foolish name, to my way of thinking. Ozzy was spotted two blocks from here on Friday night," he continued.

Hey! He must have been in my neighborhood, then! thought Bob.

"The ostrich ate the potted chrysanthemums off someone's porch, but ran off before it could be apprehended. As I hope you students are aware, ostriches can achieve speeds of up to forty miles an hour. They are also extremely powerful kickers. If the ostrich is seen, please alert me. Do *not* attempt to catch him yourselves! Thank you."

Bob's teacher, Mrs. Doubleday, shook her head in amazement. "This is really hard to believe," she said. "I feel as if I'm trapped in a Curious George book."

Suddenly she broke off. "Louie, what are you doing? You can't wear those things in here!" she exclaimed.

Louie Watson was stumbling loudly into the classroom. The reason for the stumbling—and the loudness—was that each of his feet was strapped to a concrete block with duct tape.

"But Mrs. Doubleday, it's for my science fair experiment!" he protested as he dragged himself along the floor toward his desk. He was leaving a trail of long black scrapes on the floor behind him. "See, I've attached these weights to my feet!"

"Yes, of course I see," said Mrs. Doubleday, looking as if she didn't know whether to laugh or to scream. "What are they *for?*"

"I'm trying to make myself taller!" said Louie brightly. He reached his desk and toppled heavily into his chair. "I figure if I keep having to drag these blocks around, my legs will *have* to grow! Larry's trying to make himself shorter," he added.

Just at that moment Larry Watson came stumbling into the classroom. He had somewhat smaller concrete blocks taped to the tops of his shoulders. He had had to use so much tape to make them stay on that he looked as though he was wearing a duct-tape shield. And he was staggering so much under their weight that Mrs. Doubleday had to leap forward and steady him as he pitched toward his desk.

"His blocks kind of compress him while he walks," Louie pointed out helpfully.

"We're trying to see if it's possible to make identical twins un-identical," said Larry. "Anyway, first we do the growing and shrinking process. Then we start in on the faces."

"And what are you going to do to your faces?" asked Mrs. Doubleday faintly.

"Well, we haven't really figured that out yet," Larry admitted.

"That's enough," said Mrs. Doubleday. "I don't

want to hear about it. And furthermore, you're going to have to do away with the concrete blocks. They're much too dangerous. You'll have to think up something else."

"I can tell *you're* no scientist," grumbled Larry under his breath.

"But I'm glad to see that you're all working along on your projects," Mrs. Doubleday went on. "Who else wants to talk about what they're doing for the fair?"

To poor Bob, it looked as though every hand in the room shot up except his.

Chapter Four
Bob Kelly, Boy Model

"Hey, Bob!" Jonathan called. "What are you—"

"Jonathan, I don't *know!*" said Bob in exasperation. "When are people going to stop asking me that?"

"Asking you what?" said Jonathan in a startled voice. "I was just going to ask what you were having for lunch!"

Bob relaxed a little. "Sorry, I thought you were going to ask me what I was doing for the science fair."

Four more days had passed. For Bob, they were four days in which not a single scientific idea had presented itself. Whenever anyone asked him any question that began with the words *what are you,* he felt like running away.

Luckily not everyone in his class thought about the science fair *all* the time. Tiffany Root, for instance, was extremely worried about the ostrich that had escaped from the zoo. It still hadn't been found, and Tiffany was sure it was going to sneak up from behind and attack her.

"You know, someone down the street from me was practically *killed* by that ostrich!" she fretted at lunch on Friday afternoon.

"Ozzy attacked someone?" asked Bob with interest. "I didn't hear about that! What happened?"

"Well, no one was actually hurt," Tiffany admitted, "but this family's garbage cans were knocked down. And they saw some kind of looming shape running away."

"Maybe it was a dog," Rocky Latizano suggested as he took a mammoth bite of his sandwich.

"No way! It was ten feet tall, and it had two legs! It was *definitely* the ostrich!" Tiffany shivered. "Every time I go outside, I keep thinking it's right behind me. It's going to creep up and peck me on the neck, I just know it."

"Actually, pecking's not really the problem with ostriches," said Bob as he pushed a handful of potato chips into his mouth. "Kicking is. If Ozzy kicks you, you're outta here. Ostriches can even bend iron bars."

"Oh, they can *not*," scoffed Bonnie.

"They can! I read it in the animal encyclopedia!" Bob told her.

"Well, thanks for telling Tiffany about it, anyway," said Bonnie sarcastically. "Now she has something else to worry about."

"I just can't figure out where an ostrich would be spending its time around here during the day," Diego mused as he stirred his soup. "At night, I can understand people not seeing it. But where can it hide when it gets light out? Pasadena isn't exactly the jungle!"

"I was wondering that same thing about our skunk," said Bob. "This skunk's been hanging around our garage, and we only see it in the morning and at night, never during the day. And it can't just be wandering around the neighborhood in broad daylight, even if it *is* a skunk. Someone would have seen it. And if the neighbors feel like my parents do, that skunk isn't going to have much of a future if it's captured."

Remembering how his parents had discussed calling an exterminator to deal with the skunk, Bob shook his head angrily. *I'm not going to let them get that skunk!* he said to himself. *I've just got to figure out some way to keep it away from the house, so they'll leave it alone! If only I could set up some kind of safe place for it to go. . . .*

"Why are you shaking your head and frowning like that?" Bonnie broke in. "You look like a real doofus."

Bob jumped. "Sorry," he said, embarrassed. "I was just—hey! I guess I was thinking of an idea for the science fair!"

A habitat for suburban wildlife, he said to himself excitedly. *I could follow the skunk to wherever it hides during the day, and set up a feeding station for it there. I bet other animals would start coming, too—raccoons, anyway, and maybe opossums. I could watch them, follow them around, and take pictures of them. I could do a whole presentation on how animals adapt to life in the suburbs! And it would keep the skunk away from my house!*

"I've got a really good idea!" he said aloud.

His whole lunch table burst into sarcastic applause.

"At last," said Rocky. "Now maybe you'll quit mooning around and start acting like a normal person again. Do you want your brownie?"

Bob grinned. "Yes, I do," he said. "See how back-to-normal I am?"

Unfortunately, there was no way Bob could start working on his idea during school. So when they all went back to the classroom after lunch, Bob didn't have anything to do during science. (Mrs. Doubleday had decided that until the science fair was over, she would let people work on their experiments during the time reserved for science lessons. "You'll learn at least as much as I could teach you," she had said.) And when Mrs. Doubleday realized that Bob didn't have anything to do, she told him to see if he could help any other people with their experiments.

"He can help me!" said Jennifer immediately.

"Oh, I don't think so," said Bob, even more immediately.

Jennifer's entry for the science fair was called "Homemade Makeup: Before and After." From somewhere she had managed to dig up an old pharmacist's book of makeup recipes, and she was working her way through each recipe. But concocting her own makeup was only half of Jennifer's project. She also planned to use the makeup to do makeovers on people. That was the before-and-after part.

Bob didn't want anything to do with either part.

"I don't see why you can't help Jennifer," said Mrs. Doubleday briskly. "You go and give her a hand, now."

Bob stared goggle-eyed at his teacher. She wasn't trying to tease him, was she? "Boys don't do stuff with *makeup!*" he choked out.

"Now, now, Bob," said Mrs. Doubleday. "Let's not have any stereotypes in my classroom. Learning a little bit about makeup won't hurt you."

She walked away before Bob could answer.

"Okay, then," said Jennifer happily. She took Bob by the sleeve and pulled him firmly toward her desk.

Spread out on the desk were rows and rows of bottles, jars, and tubes. There were bright-red powders and hot-pink pellets. There were eye-droppers filled with brownish gunk and squares of wax in tin cans. There was tincture of benzoin, potassium carbonate, something called extract of neroli, and something else called peru balsam. Jennifer didn't usually get too involved in school projects, but she had really been busy with this one.

Bob was impressed in spite of himself. "Where did you get all this stuff?" he asked.

"Oh, the drugstore. And some mail-order places," Jennifer told him. She was leafing through a sheaf of recipes as she spoke. "Here. We're going to make some skin cream first. Mrs. Doubleday said I could use the hot plate."

"Hey, no way!" protested Junior Smith. "I need the hot plate for my popcorn!"

Bob looked up to see Junior bent double over the weight of the huge bag of unpopped popcorn he was carrying. "How much do you have there?" he asked.

"Thirty-five pounds. It only cost a dollar-fifty! Can you believe it?" said Junior proudly. "I'm doing an experiment on how to make a profit mass-producing popcorn." He dumped the heavy bag onto Bob's desk with a sigh of relief and pulled a little notebook from his back pocket. "I figure I can make about three hundred bushels for five dollars," he said, flipping through the notebook. "Then I can put all the popcorn into sandwich bags and sell each bag for seventy-five cents. That's a clear profit of—let me see—"

"Well, you're not making *any* profit popping it on the hot plate," Jennifer interrupted. "I need the hot plate for my makeup. Mrs. Doubleday *said*."

Mrs. Doubleday was walking over to them now. "What's going on, guys?" she asked.

Jennifer and Junior both started talking at once.

"You *said* I could—"

"I've got to pop this stuff *somewhere*—"

"Hey, hold on! Wait a minute!" protested Mrs. Doubleday. "Junior, Jennifer's right. I did tell her she could use the hot plate. How about if I call Ms. Weinstock and see if you can use the microwave in the lunchroom? Microwaving is a great way to do popcorn, and you'd be able to get it done a lot faster."

In a second she was back. "Ms. Weinstock says it's fine," she reported. "She says she's got some bags you can pop it in, too."

Junior picked up the sack of popcorn and lugged it away, and Jennifer turned back to her work with a sigh of satisfaction. She picked up a few containers and led Bob over to the counter, where a hot plate was plugged in and waiting for her. "Okay, the first thing we need to do is put some Vaseline into this pot." She scooped out a clump with a spoon.

"Hey, that looks good! Can I have a taste?"

It was Rocky Latizano—and he wasn't kidding.

"Rocky, it's *Vaseline!*" said Bob.

"Oh. Well, call me if you make anything that looks edible."

"Okay, now we have to melt in some paraffin," said Jennifer. She dropped a square of grayish wax into the pot. "And some lanolin." She squeezed two inches of pale-yellow ointment out of a tube. "And now we just stir it all together until it's smooth."

The Vaseline was the first to melt, and then the lanolin. But the square of paraffin just bumped and clanked around the pot as they stirred it. It didn't seem to be softening at all.

Jennifer clicked her tongue impatiently. "This is going to take longer than I thought. What can we do while we—I know! Let me try out some of the stuff I've already made!"

She darted back to her desk and returned with

another armful of bottles and jars. "We can try the blush and lip gloss, at least," she said. "I've got the formulas pretty well finished for those."

Bob eyed her uneasily. "You want me to put that stuff on you? I don't know if I can."

"Oh, no," said Jennifer. "I want to put it on *you*. How else am I going to see how it looks?"

"But Jennifer, I can't wear makeup!" gasped Bob in a whisper.

"Oh, come on," said Jennifer. "Remember what Mrs. Doubleday said? Just try it on for one second. Then you can wash it all off."

And before Bob could think of a good answer, she had picked up a jar of pinkish stuff and put dots of it all over his face. She rubbed them in vigorously, then stepped back and stared intently at Bob.

"Good," she said at last. "Let's try some eyeshadow now." She smeared slimy blue stuff all over Bob's eyelids.

"Okay, I can see that I've got to change the formula for the lip gloss," she said a few minutes later as she carefully outlined Bob's mouth in flaming red. "It's not spreading very well. Maybe some glycerin would—"

Brrrriiiing! Brrrriiiing! Brrrriiiing! Brrrriiiing!

"Oh, dear," said Mrs. Doubleday in dismay. "I didn't know that we were supposed to have a fire drill today."

"No, it's great!" cried Jennifer. "Now I'll get to see what my makeup looks like in natural light!"

"Fine, dear," Mrs. Doubleday said distractedly. "Now, unplug the hot plate and put the pot in the sink. Let's line up, everyone!"

"Wait a minute!" called Bob. "I've got to wash my face!"

"I'm sorry, but that will have to wait," said Mrs. Doubleday. She clapped her hands sharply. "Come on, everyone! Let's go!"

There was just enough time for Bob to catch a glimpse of himself in the little mirror hanging by the coat rack.

He almost passed out on the spot.

I look like a clown! he thought in horror. *I can't go out onto the playground in front of everyone!*

"Hey, that's very becoming, Bob," said Larry Watson with an evil grin.

"Nice look, dude!" chortled Rocky as they filed out into the hall.

"Don't worry," said Jennifer calmly. "Just think how helpful you're being to my science-fair project."

But somehow that didn't make Bob feel any better.

Luckily no one's mind was on makeup when they got outside. Instead, everyone was watching the lunchroom. Something unusual seemed to be going on inside.

And something unusual seemed to be coming outside, too—popcorn. A blizzard of it was flying out of the lunchroom window onto the lawn. And if you looked into the window—as everyone kept trying to do while Mr. Haypence kept trying to shoo them away—you could see that an avalanche of popcorn was pouring out of the open door of the walk-in microwave.

"Is this what triggered the fire-alarm system?" Mr. Haypence thundered angrily at Ms. Weinstock, who was standing next to him.

"I guess so," she replied in a dazed voice. "But I had no idea that Junior would try to pop all of it at once!"

Mr. Haypence turned to Junior, who was standing next to Ms. Weinstock. "Well, young man, I'm waiting to hear your explanation for this," he said in an ominous voice.

Junior cleared his throat and turned to the crowd. "Before I explain, let me just ask if anyone would like to buy a little popcorn," he said. "As you can all see, it's fresh-popped. And I'll give you a special deal if you pick it up off the lawn yourself."

Chapter Five

Bob in the Wild

Bob usually slept late on Saturdays, but that Saturday morning he was up before anyone else in the family. If the skunk came to call on the Kellys' garbage cans, he wanted to be ready.

It was six o'clock when he tiptoed into the kitchen, grabbed a box of cereal, and slipped quietly out the back door. The dawn air was fresh and sweet-smelling, and the birds were just starting to wake up. It was a great morning for tracking down skunks.

The Kellys never actually used their garage for their cars. There was too much other stuff in there: bags of fertilizer, four rakes, the gas grill, the lawn mower, a few lawn chairs, and a rowing machine that Bob's father had gotten for Christmas six years before and used only twice. For a garage, it was crowded. For hiding from a skunk, it was perfect.

Bob walked quietly to a spot behind the lawn mower and sat down to wait. For half an hour he sat there, sleepily eating cereal out of the box. Finally, just when he was about to give up and go back inside, he heard a cautious rustling near the garage door.

He leaned forward and craned his neck around the lawn mower. Yes, it was the skunk. It was sniffing around the garbage cans in its usual unhurried way, swishing its tail gently in the air.

The skunk stood up on its hind legs and scrabbled at one of the garbage cans hopefully. Of course, nothing happened. It cast a wistful glance up toward the top of the can. Then it dropped to all fours, sniffed around for a few more seconds, and slowly started out of the garage.

Bob had been sitting for so long that his joints creaked as he stood up. At the sound, the skunk glanced around sharply, and Bob ducked back down behind the lawn mower. But the skunk didn't seem to see him. It waddled down the driveway and out to the street. Bob tiptoed after it.

Tail fluttering gently in the breeze, the skunk

trotted along the sidewalk past the Kellys' next-door neighbor's house, and past the house after that. But at the next house, which belonged to a family named the Ogdens, the skunk turned and ambled up toward the driveway toward the Ogdens' garage.

Oh, no! Bob thought. *I didn't realize he went to other houses, too!*

What am I going to do? he wondered. *I can't follow him into the Ogdens' yard! I'd better just wait here on the sidewalk.*

The Ogdens must have had great garbage. The skunk stayed there for what seemed like hours while Bob waited impatiently on the sidewalk. After a few minutes, a car swooped down the street. It slowed down when it passed Bob. *Are they watching me?* Bob wondered uneasily. *After all, it's not that common to see a twelve-year-old boy sitting on the sidewalk at the crack of dawn! But no one would believe me if I told them the truth. . . .*

It was almost seven o'clock when at last the skunk padded out of the Ogdens' yard, licking its chops. That time it didn't walk down to the sidewalk, though. Instead it glanced around quickly and darted into the bushes in front of the Ogdens' house.

Does it hide out in there? Bob wondered. *I'm not going to get much of a habitat study going if—*

But then he saw the skunk's tail moving through the bushes. The skunk crept slowly along the front of the house until it reached the edge of the yard. Then it bolted across the driveway and into the bushes in front of the next house. It continued on in that way until it reached the end of the block.

It must get shyer as it gets lighter, Bob thought as he followed the skunk along. *Well, that makes sense.*

"Morning, Bob!" a voice boomed behind him. It was old Dr. Mayhew from down the block, with his ancient dachsund Tweeter. "Taking your constitutional?" he asked jovially, his voice blasting the peaceful day.

Bob gave him a big, fake smile. "Uh-huh," he said. *What's a constitutional?* he thought.

I hope Tweeter doesn't see the skunk! he thought even harder.

"Well, keep up the good work!" shouted Mr. Mayhew. To Bob's relief, he and Tweeter lumbered away without any more questions.

Bob checked his watch again. It was ten after seven, and people were probably starting to wake up in lots of the houses. Bob's imagination started to work. *They'd see him creeping slowly down their street and peering into their bushes,* he thought. *And then Bob's parents would get a call from the police station, where Bob would have been taken after someone had him arrested for attempted robbery.*

Luckily the skunk was really starting to move along. It dashed across the street, raced toward another clump of bushes on the next block, and zipped through. It passed house after house and finally reached the end of the next block. The skunk turned right, dashed across another street, and kept going.

It's heading for Indian Hills, Bob realized.

The Indian Hills Country Club was only a few blocks from Bob's house, behind a street filled with houses that were about three times as big as the ones on Bob's street. Those big houses had a wonderful view of the club's golf course, which looked very lush and inviting with its glossy greens surrounded by picturesque woods. Bob had played there a lot when he was little (and when there weren't any golfers around), but he hadn't thought about the golf course in years.

Indian Hills was separated from the road by a narrow gully with a creek at the bottom. That was where the skunk was headed. It scurried through the stone pillars on either side of the club's main entrance, ducked down into the gully, and disappeared into the weeds.

Bob followed it through the main entrance, and saw a huge blue sign in the middle of the drive.

CAUTION! PROCEED NO FARTHER!
UNDER CONSTRUCTION
WALTER JOHNSON, BUILDERS
CLOSED UNTIL FURTHER NOTICE

So Indian Hills is closed, thought Bob. *No wonder the skunk spends its days here.*

He kept his head low as he stepped cautiously into the gully. *I bet lots of animals come here,* he said to himself as he followed the creek. *It's the perfect place for suburban wildlife!*

The golf course was just coming into sight now, and Bob could see the strip of woods behind it. He could also see the skunk's black-and-white flag of a tail just ahead of him.

What he didn't see was the end of the stick he stepped on. At least he didn't see it until he stepped on it and it snapped loudly in half.

"Ouch!" Bob said aloud. The broken end of the stick had just jabbed him in the ankle.

There was a sudden rustling in the weeds about a foot in front of Bob, and the skunk popped its head out to see what was going on. It leaped back fearfully when it saw Bob. Then it stamped its feet.

It was stamping them in an awfully *meaningful* way.

No, thought Bob. *Don't!*

But before he could even turn to run, the skunk was wheeling around and taking aim.

"Bob! What happened to you?" Mrs. Kelly gasped in horror fifteen minutes later as Bob opened the back door and stumbled into the kitchen. She was all the way at the other end of the room, but news travels fast when someone's just been sprayed by a skunk.

"I found out where the skunk lives," Bob answered sheepishly.

"You go right back outside," Mrs. Kelly ordered, her voice somewhat muffled by the dish-towel she was holding over her nose. She tossed a towel and a big garbage bag to Bob. "Go hose yourself off in the backyard," she ordered him through the towel. "Then take off your clothes in the garage and wrap the towel around yourself. Put the clothes in this bag and knot it up. Double-knot it! Throw it away. Come in and take a shower. And then come back down so you can tell me exactly what's going on—and so I can throttle you."

So much for keeping this project a secret, Bob said to himself.

"Don't you have any tomato juice?" he asked helpfully through the door. "I read that tomato juice is supposed to be good for getting rid of skunk odor."

The door banged in his face.

Despite what had happened, Bob was back at the golf course that same evening, right at the edge of the woods. And he had brought suburban-wildlife food with him, a whole shopping bag full.

The sun was just touching the horizon as Bob opened the bag and began scattering its contents around in the open. First came a few carrots, then some grapefruit segments. (Bob didn't know if any animals liked grapefruits, but there had been a whole bowlful in the refrigerator, so he had figured he might as well try them.) Then a box of raisins, some lettuce, a torn-up loaf of oatmeal bread, some chopped apples, some cubes of Swiss cheese, a can of cat food left over from the time Bob had taken care of his uncle's cat, a few handfuls of stale pumpkin seeds left over from Halloween, and—last of all—some marsh-mallows.

The marshmallows had been Lynn's idea after he had told his family about his project. "Marsh-mallows are my favorite food! Why wouldn't an animal like them?" she had demanded. "If that skunk goes around eating garbage, it's got to like marshmallows," she added practically.

Bob selected a carrot for himself and then walked back to the edge of the woods, where he concealed himself behind a large tree.

It was starting to get dark, but Bob didn't need

his flashlight yet. There was nothing to see, anyway. Bob took a bite of carrot and settled back on his elbows. He could hear the creek rushing along, and the crickets were just starting to chirp.

Ten minutes passed.

It's been a long day, Bob thought with an enormous yawn. *Maybe I should just leave this stuff here. I could come back tomorrow morning early to see whether anything has—*

Then he heard a rustling noise right behind him.

Bob sat motionless.

About five feet to his left, a raccoon was walking out of the woods. It was so close Bob could hear it sniffing.

The raccoon padded carefully out onto the golf course. It was starting to walk away when it suddenly noticed the food. It stopped short, and sniffed the air again. Then it moved slowly toward the feast spread out on the grass. It picked up a marshmallow, looked at it curiously, and put it down again. Then it picked up a chunk of cat food in its little black paws and began nibbling at it.

Trying to move as quietly as possible, Bob picked up the notebook he'd brought with him. "Raccoon—cat food," he wrote down. "Resisted marshmallows."

Not more than five minutes had gone by before the raccoon had company—an opossum. The opossum also bypassed Lynn's marshmallows, and seemed more interested in the cheese.

I'd better bring more main course–type things tomorrow, Bob thought. *Some hard-boiled eggs, maybe.* "Opossum—cheese," he wrote.

When the raccoon had finished the cat food, it walked slowly away. Two rabbits came out of the woods soon afterward, and were just starting in on the carrots when there was a crashing sound in the woods.

Something—or someone—was walking toward Bob. Something person-sized. Bob turned around quickly, but the woods were too dark to see anything.

I bet it's someone from the country club, thought Bob with a sinking heart. *They're coming to kick me off the property. Or it could just be a guard who's patrolling this block. If I sit very still, maybe no one will see me.*

The rabbits and the opossum looked up sharply. Then, to Bob's surprise, they returned to their suppers.

Crackle. Crackle. Crash. The sounds were coming closer.

It can't be a person, Bob said to himself. *The animals would be scared if it were. Maybe it's a deer.*

He turned around again, just as a huge, dark shape came looming out of the woods.

"I don't believe it," Bob whispered.

An ostrich was walking toward him.

Chapter Six

How to Hide an Ostrich

"Ozzy?" asked Bob in a whisper.

At the sound of his name, the ostrich turned around and stared beadily at Bob. Bob didn't move a muscle. He could hardly breathe. He was paralyzed with amazement.

Like most people, Bob had never sat within patting range of an ostrich. And even when he'd visited the zoo, he had never paid much attention to the ostriches. He couldn't believe how big Ozzy was.

He's taller than my father! he marveled. *I bet I only come up to his shoulder—if that's what it's called on an ostrich!*

Ozzy was half ugly and half cute. His legs were long, bare, and spindly-looking, like giant, extra-bony chicken drumsticks. He had two dinosaurish toes on each foot. His body was covered with black feathers except for his wings and tail, which were tipped with beautiful, curling white plumes. His long neck had a skimpy coating of short, stubbly white feathers. And his bright eyes were only a few inches from Bob's.

You don't know it, Ozzy, Bob told him silently, *but I just found a new science-fair project: you. As long as I can keep you secret. And as long as you don't try to kick me.*

But Ozzy didn't seem to have any intention of kicking Bob. Ostrich and boy stared at each other for what must have been thirty seconds. Suddenly Ozzy seemed to decide that he had nothing to be afraid of. He turned away and stalked out onto the golf course.

Then, like the animals that had come before him, he caught sight of the food Bob had spread out on the golf course. Ozzy gave a little squeak—a very small sound for such a big bird—and bounded forward. He didn't stop to make up his mind about what kind of food he wanted, either. The marshmallows were closest, and he started in on them. When they were all gone, he dived into the pumpkin seeds. At first he had a little trouble picking the seeds up out of the grass, but he managed. And when the seeds were gone, he began to gobble down the carrots that the rabbits had left.

He must have been starving! Bob realized. *It's been at least a week since he escaped, and he's got a big stomach to fill. I wonder what he's been living on all this time?*

Ozzy finished the carrots and dipped his long neck toward the food again. Then he paused. Maybe he wasn't hungry any longer, or maybe he didn't like the rest of the food there. Whatever the reason, he lifted his head, turned to look at Bob once more, and then walked with stately steps back into the woods. It was too dark for Bob to see which way he went once he was in the underbrush.

I'll have to come back and look for him tomorrow, Bob thought. *And I'll try to come up with some other food. Marshmallows can't be very good for him.*

Bob stood up, stretched, and glanced at his watch. It was almost eight o'clock. He had told his parents he'd be home by eight. If he hurried, he would just make it.

And the earlier he went to bed that night, the earlier he could come back the next day.

"Bob!"

Bob blinked and looked around. Mrs. Doubleday was staring strangely at him from the front of the room. "Uh, did you say something, Mrs. Doubleday?" he asked her.

"I certainly did. Your name, and several times, too," she told him. "I guess you didn't hear me."

"I guess not. Sorry."

He had been thinking about Ozzy.

"Well, I was telling your classmates that Ms. Wu is going to be visiting our classroom today. She's going from class to class checking everyone's project for the science fair so that she can work up a press release for the newspapers. So I'd like each of you to write up a brief description of your project for her. Then you can start working on your experiments. Ms. Wu will be here in about half an hour. Yes, Tiffany?"

"Will our descriptions be graded?" Tiffany asked.

"No, Tiffany," said Mrs. Doubleday patiently. Then she turned to Bob again. "Bob, you *do* have an experiment now, right?"

"Right," said Bob.

But I'm not going to tell Ms. Wu about it, he thought.

He took two sheets of paper out of his desk.

Now, let's see, he thought. *I have to write two different descriptions. One is for Ms. Wu. I'll make that one as boring as possible. The other one will be about Ozzy. No one will see that until the day of the science fair.*

On the first piece of paper, Bob wrote, "Purpose: To create a feeding station for suburban wildlife."

On the other, he wrote, "Purpose: To create a habitat where an escaped ostrich can feel at home."

On the first piece of paper, Bob quickly listed the animals he'd seen on the golf course and what they'd eaten.

On the second piece of paper, he wrote, "I have been observing Ozzy for two days now. On the first day, he ate marshmallows, pumpkin seeds, and carrots. On the second day, he ate peanuts, grapes, and one miniature pecan pie for breakfast. For supper, he ate tomatoes, a piece of whole-wheat pita bread, and four apples. I don't think he got enough to eat. I'll bring him more food from now on."

I'd better be careful about that, he thought. I don't want Mom and Dad to get suspicious about the kind of animal I'm feeding, after all. Mom said she doesn't mind my taking stuff like bread crumbs and lettuce, but she'll definitely notice if I start taking ostrich-type food. She's already mad that I lost the salt shaker.

He bent down to the paper again. "Ozzy is already getting tamer. Living at the zoo has probably made him pretty used to people. He recognizes his name and looks at me whenever

I call him. He won't come when I call yet, but he does let me pat him.

"Yesterday morning I arrived at Ozzy's habitat"—Bob didn't want to say where that was, in case anyone found his description—"while he was still sleeping. He sleeps at the edge of the woods in a little hollow he scraped out with his foot. He was resting his head on a fallen branch when I saw him."

Bob stopped for a second. He wanted to write, "He looked like a sleeping baby," but he didn't. Even though it was true, it sounded too mushy.

"This week I plan to learn as much as I can about ostriches so that I can make Ozzy as happy in his habitat as he would be in the wild."

Once again Bob put down his pen.

Could I really keep Ozzy? he wondered. *I kind of feel as if he belonged to me already. But is it illegal not to take him back to the zoo?*

No, he told himself stubbornly. *Ozzy doesn't belong in the zoo. He can't possibly be happy all cooped up there. He's much better off where he is, with me taking care of him. I won't worry about it.*

"Good morning, everybody!"

Ms. Wu came tap-tap-tapping into the room on her high heels. There was a huge sheaf of papers in her hand.

"Hard at work, I see!" she trilled. "Don't let me disturb you. I'm just going to come around and ask a few questions about what you're doing."

Ms. Wu stopped at Rocky's desk first. "Can you tell me a little bit about your project, dear?" she asked.

"Sure," said Rocky. He picked up a jar of marshmallow fluff and took off the lid. "It's called, 'All About'—"

"Just a minute," Ms. Wu interrupted. "Does your teacher allow you to eat in class?" She glanced over at Mrs. Doubleday.

Mrs. Doubleday gave her a weary nod. "It's part of his project," she said. "In a weak moment I let him con me into it."

"See, my project is called 'All About Calories,'" Rocky explained. As he talked, he was scooping fingerfuls of marshmallow fluff straight out of the jar. "I'm trying to see how many calories I can eat between now and the science fair. It's been very interesting because I've been learning a lot about how many calories there are in different foods. For instance, I was eating an apple at the beginning of the experiment, and suddenly I thought, I'd better look this up in the calorie book! So I did, and can you believe it? An apple has only a hundred calories! I mean, in less than the amount of time it takes me to eat

65

an apple, I could be eating a candy bar for three hundred calories. Or a stick of butter for eight hundred calories! I haven't eaten a whole stick of butter," he added. "Not yet. But I'm working up to it. You have to train for this kind of thing, you know."

"I see," said Ms. Wu. "Well, that's a very, ah, unusual idea."

"First prize, you think?" asked Rocky. He tilted the jar of marshmallow fluff so he could stare into it. "You know, if I could heat this stuff up," he said thoughtfully, "I'd be able to drink it. Then I wouldn't have to waste so much time scooping it out."

With a shudder Ms. Wu quickly moved on to the next desk, which happened to be Louie Watson's. "And what are you—what happened to you?"

Louie's nose was completely covered with Band-Aids, and he was holding his arms up over his head.

"Dothig's the badder," he said thickly. "I'b tryig to squash dowd by dose, that's all."

"Squash down your nose! Whatever for?" gasped Ms. Wu.

"He wants to change the way it looks," Larry Watson called from across the room. As he walked toward them, Ms. Wu could see that Larry's nose was under construction, too. Only

Larry's method was simpler. He was just using his finger to push the tip of his nose as far back as it would go. He looked like he was doing a very bad imitation of a pig.

"See, we're un-identicalizing ourselves," Larry explained, without moving his finger. "Every few days we add a new method. Now we're working on our noses. We were using concrete blocks to change our height, but *she* said"—he glanced resentfully at Mrs. Doubleday—"that it wasn't good for our spines, so Louie is trying to stretch himself out by keeping his arms up. It's a lot harder, though," he added with another baleful look in his teacher's direction. "We're going to have to think of another way."

"Toborrow we're goig to start changig our ears," put in Louie.

"How?" asked Ms. Wu, a little fearfully.

"Oh, little weights, or something," said Larry blithely.

Ms. Wu opened and shut her mouth a few times without any sound coming out. "My, this class has so many interesting ideas!" she said at last. "I can tell you're really going for it!" But she didn't say it with her usual conviction.

By the time she got to Bob's desk, though, Ms. Wu was looking a lot more cheerful. She had heard about Diego's glycoprotein-synthesizing project and about Bonnie and Tilly's bees. She had also been given a makeover by Jennifer—"a *free* makeover," Jennifer had reminded her. (Bob had to admit that Jennifer had done a pretty good job, only he thought the lip gloss still wasn't smooth enough.)

"Now, let's see what you're doing," she said to Bob. "I'm sure it's a neat idea!"

What Bob was doing at the moment was learning that one ostrich egg weighs as much as forty hen's eggs. He didn't mention that, though. He just closed the animal encyclopedia and handed Ms. Wu his first project description. That was the fake one.

" 'I am putting out food for wild animals,' " Ms. Wu read aloud. (Bob had been careful to write as boringly as he could.) " 'So far, I have seen two rabbits, an opossum, and some other animals. They seem to like the food.' "

She looked at Bob, then read the rest of the description silently. "Well!" she said brightly when she'd finished reading the description. "Isn't this, uh ... And your handwriting is so neat, too!"

She handed the sheet of paper back to Bob. "But you know, dear, you might try to make it a *little* more exciting. The way you've written it now, I'm afraid there's not much that would get people's attention. I don't want to hurt your feelings, but—"

"Oh, it's okay," said Bob quickly.

And to himself, he thought, *It's great. The less attention I attract, the better.*

I don't want anyone noticing me until the day I walk Ozzy into the lunchroom.

Chapter Seven

Ozzy and Bonnie Sittin' in a Tree...

"Okay, let's try it one more time," said Bob. He patted the ostrich on the neck, backed away about twenty feet, and called, "Ozzy! Come! Come here, Ozzy!"

Ozzy eyed him coyly. Then he put one foot forward, tapped the ground a couple of times, and walked up to Bob.

"That's great!" Bob told him excitedly. He patted Ozzy's long neck and handed him a miniature pecan pie. "You're really learning! Tomorrow we'll try it with a leash. And when the science fair comes, I bet you'll be all trained!"

Ozzy wasn't paying any attention. He finished his pie and nudged Bob's hand with his beak.

"Okay, boy. You can have one more," said Bob.

He reached into his pocket and pulled out another miniature pecan pie. It was a little squashed, but Ozzy never seemed to care about that. "No more, though. Not until tonight. We don't want you getting fat."

He began walking toward the woods. "I've got to go to school now, Oz. Let's get you back to your nest."

"Nest" was a polite word for it. As Bob had written in his description, it was really just a dip in the ground that Ozzy had scratched out with his foot. But Ozzy seemed comfortable there. At least he always went there willingly enough when Bob had to leave.

Bob scattered some chickpeas around the nest. Besides miniature pecan pies, chickpeas seemed to be Ozzy's favorite food. "Now, no wandering around while I'm in school, okay?" he said. "We don't want anyone spotting you. Not when there are only two more weeks before the science fair."

Bob gave Ozzy's neck another pat and walked back out onto the golf course. He had twenty minutes to get to school, which would only be enough if he ran all the way.

He was sprinting the last block toward the school when he suddenly realized that Bonnie was a few feet ahead of him. "Hey, Bon!" he called, slowing to a walk. "Wait up!"

Bonnie turned around to see who was calling.

She didn't look incredibly happy when she realized that it was Bob.

Uh-oh, thought Bob. *She's mad. I guess I should have told her I wouldn't be walking to school with her today, and yesterday, and the day before that. Since I'm at the golf course every day after supper, I just keep forgetting to call.*

"Oh, hi," Bonnie said coldly. "What's new?"

"Not much," said Bob. "Haven't seen you in a while!"

"That's your fault, not mine," said Bonnie. "*You're* the one who can't walk to school anymore."

"But Bonnie, you know I have to check up on my wildlife every morning!" Bob protested.

Bonnie gave him a scornful glance. "You can't tell me that dumping some rabbit chow out in a field somewhere takes that long! How many animals do you have to keep track of? A couple of rabbits and a skunk! What's the big deal?"

"Well, I have to take notes on them, too," said Bob. "That takes a lot of time! C'mon, Bon. We can walk to school together once the science fair is over!"

Bonnie really looked scornful then. "Bob, what kind of drip do you think I am? I don't care about the walking-to-school part! I care that you don't even trust me enough to tell me what your project's about! I thought we were supposed to be friends!"

"Don't talk so loudly!" Bob begged her. Then he realized how suspicious that sounded. "I mean, of course I trust you! I've already told you what my project's about!" he said in as sincere a voice as he could manage.

"Right," Bonnie snapped. "That's why you spend all your time reading books about Africa during science-project time. Get real, Bob! You may be able to fool Ms. Wu, but you can't fool me!"

And she swept off toward the schoolyard.

Keeping Ozzy secret from Bonnie was tough, but keeping him secret from Bob's parents was almost impossible. Bob didn't have much trouble explaining why he was out of the house so often. His parents were delighted to know that he was studying wildlife, although Mrs. Kelly did say, "But if you ever tussle with that skunk again, I'm getting Mr. Haypence to put you back into first grade." But the problems with Ozzy's food were a lot harder to explain away.

"I'm going out to the supermarket, Bob," his mother told him one evening, poking her head into his bedroom. "Anything you want to add to the list?"

"Sure!" said Bob, a little too quickly. "Let's see, we could use some orange juice. Also some chicken nuggets, and some kind of cookies."

"O. J. Chicken nuggets. Cookies," his mother repeated as she wrote it all down.

"Oh, and could you maybe pick up some grapes? We haven't had any grapes in ages."

"Bunch of grapes," said his mother slowly as she wrote it down.

"Well, uh, how about three bunches? Or five?" suggested Bob. "Lynn likes grapes a lot, too."

So did Ozzy, of course.

Mrs. Kelly stared at Bob for a second.

"Okay. *Two* bunches of grapes," she wrote at last.

"And—oh, yeah! I almost forgot!" Bob said casually. "Could you pick up a couple of cans of chickpeas and about fifteen miniature pecan pies or so? For snacks?"

Mrs. Kelly put down her pencil and stared at her son.

"You don't *like* chickpeas," she said suspiciously.

"I do now! I love them!" protested Bob. "You know, I am growing up, Mom. I don't eat just kid foods any more. I'm starting to like more sophisticated stuff now!"

"Like miniature pecan pies, I suppose?"

"Well, Mom, I've got to have some kind of dessert after all those chickpeas!" Bob said weakly.

His mother didn't seem convinced.

"Something is happening to all the food in this

house, Bob," she said. "And I've got a feeling it's going to that skunk of yours."

Bob didn't have to lie about that, at least.

"I swear it's not going to the skunk, Mom!" he exclaimed.

"Well, it's not all going into you," said his mother skeptically. "If it was, you'd probably weigh two hundred pounds by now. Even if it's not going to skunks—and I think it is—you can use your own allowance to pay for that kind of food."

At that point, Bob decided it would be a good idea to change the subject.

"You know, Mom, that reminds me," he said. "I've been meaning to tell you that my allowance is much, much too small."

Bob's mother didn't exactly go for that idea, so he decided he'd have to start begging. "Anyone have anything they don't want to eat?" he asked at lunch the next day. "Chantilly, those cookies look kind of dry. You don't want them, do you?"

Chantilly just stared at him. "Are you really Rocky wearing a Bob disguise?" she asked. "Of course I want these cookies! They're not dry!"

"Well, how about your hot-dog roll, then?" asked Bob. "You don't really need it."

"I *want* it, though!" protested Chantilly. "What's your problem, Bob? You've been acting awfully weird lately."

"Oh, no problem," said Bob quickly. "I'm just hungry—you know?"

"If you're really hungry, have I got a deal for you!" said Junior Smith enthusiastically. "Seventeen Hefty bags of popcorn—for the low, low price of just five dollars!"

Unfortunately for Junior, no one in school had seemed interested in buying stale popcorn at the prices he had hoped for. So two days ago he had switched his experiment to a study of price-slashing.

And that was how Ozzie began eating popcorn.

As the days went by, the thing that made it hardest for Bob to keep Ozzy a secret was Ozzy himself.

Ozzy was becoming tamer and tamer. He would come when Bob called his name. He would let Bob pat him. By the time two weeks had passed, he even let Bob put a leash around his neck and lead him along the edge of the golf course.

Yes, Ozzy was behaving better and better—but he was also becoming more and more listless. When he wasn't performing for Bob, he sat around droopily, staring into space. Sometimes it took him three tries before he could heave himself off his nest, and sometimes he'd stop walking or eating to give Bob a look that could

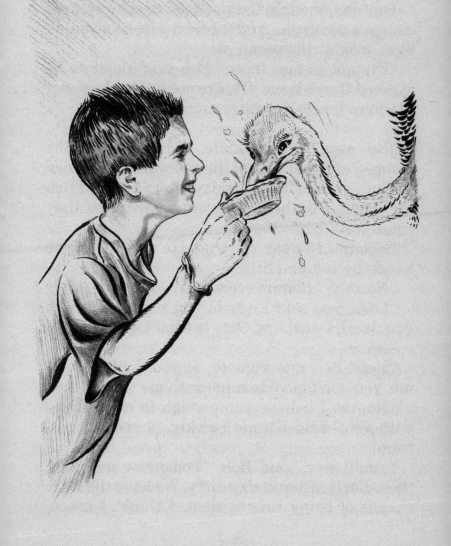

only be reproachful. For a while Bob was afraid he was sick, but Ozzy didn't show any other symptoms.

One day, though, Ozzy refused to eat anything except a pecan pie. And the next day, he wouldn't even look at the pecan pie.

"I've got to face facts," Bob said aloud as he stroked Ozzy's neck. "You're not happy. I wonder if you're lonely for other ostriches?"

"No way," said Bonnie incredulously. She stopped in the middle of the sidewalk and turned to stare at Bob. It was Friday afternoon, and Bob had waited by her locker after school so they could walk home together.

"Bonnie, I swear it's true. He's living in the woods by Indian Hills."

"No way," Bonnie repeated.

"Look, you said I was hiding something from you. Well, I was! And Ozzy is what I was hiding!"

"No w—"

"*Yes*," Bob interrupted. "If you don't believe me, you don't have to come with me to see him."

"No, no. I believe you enough to come along with you," said Bonnie quickly. "I just—an *ostrich?*"

"You'll see," said Bob. "Tomorrow morning, then. Early, around six-thirty. We have the least chance of being caught then, I think. I mean,

Indian Hills is closed, but you never know when a couple of golf addicts might suddenly decide they *had* to play a few holes."

"Six-thirty is fine," said Bonnie. "I'll be sitting on my front porch."

"Great, Bonnie!" said Bob happily. "There's one thing, though. When we find Ozzy, I want you to wear this mask I made for you."

"A mask? Why? Does he peck?"

"Well, it's not exactly a protective mask," Bob said slowly. "It's made out of papier-mâché. It's more of a—well, an ostrich mask."

"An *ostrich mask?*" Bonnie shrieked. "Why would I want to wear an ostrich mask?"

"Well, I think he's lonely for other ostriches. But he already knows me," Bob explained simply, "and he won't take me seriously if I come in wearing the mask. It has to be someone he hasn't seen before."

That was how, the next morning, Bonnie was introduced to Ozzy in an ostrich mask.

"I feel ridiculous in this thing!" she complained as Bob led her along the gully toward the golf course. Her papier-mâché head was bobbing in the air about three feet above her real head, and her eyes were glaring out of the mask's neck.

"You look great," Bob said absent-mindedly.

He was trying to see Ozzy in the underbrush. "Oh, there he is!"

Ozzy was lying limply in his shabby nest as Bob and Bonnie walked toward him. His eyes were half-closed, and his head was drooping dejectedly onto a pile of sticks.

Bonnie gasped. "You weren't kidding!" she cried ecstatically. "Oh, Bob, he's so cute! I love him! Can I pat him?"

"Wait a sec," said Bob. "Let me get his attention first. We don't want to startle him."

He whistled softly. "Ozzy!" he called.

Ozzy's eyelids fluttered, but he didn't move.

"Ozzy! Hey, Oz!" called Bob. He tossed a miniature pecan pie toward the ostrich. It landed about five inches from his beak.

Ozzy still didn't stir.

"Is he okay?" Bonnie asked in a whisper. "He looks kind of tired or something."

"He's been acting like that a lot recently," Bob told her. "You try calling him. Maybe a different voice will wake him up."

Bonnie cleared her throat nervously. "Um, Ozzy?" she squeaked.

Bonnie must have sounded more like a bird than Bob did. At any rate, Ozzy opened his eyes and lifted his head.

When he saw Bonnie, he let out a hiss of excitement. He clambered to his feet, gulped down the miniature pecan pie that Bob had thrown him, and rushed over to Bonnie. He gave her a loving buffet with his head that knocked her off her feet.

It was ostrich-love at first sight.

Chapter Eight

Ozzy's Rendezvous with Destiny

"All right, everyone!" called Ms. Wu. "Let's move on into the lunchroom and hit those booths!"

"Quiet in the halls, please," said a passing teacher, and Ms. Wu blushed. "Sorry," she said.

Everyone who was planning to participate in the science fair was standing in the hall outside the lunchroom, clutching the stuff they'd need to set up their booths. That meant all forty-eight sixth graders, twenty of the fifth graders, sixteen fourth graders, eight third graders, three second graders, two first graders, and one kindergarten boy who was holding nothing but a balloon with a face drawn on it were crowded together in the hall.

Mr. Haypence held up his arms. "In the name of Science Awareness Month, let the science begin!"

One second, it seemed, ninety-eight Hollis students were standing just outside the lunchroom. The next second, all ninety-eight of them were milling around inside the lunchroom. And Mr. Haypence was somewhere under their feet.

No, he had raced to the lunchroom stage, where he was standing bellowing out instructions that no one was paying any attention to.

"I've got to have a booth by the window!" Bob heard Jennifer calling shrilly. "My makeup needs lots of natural light to look good!"

Tilly went dashing in front of Bob with a big wooden box—a beehive, Bob guessed. "Bonnie, don't forget that we need to make some kind of pipeline for the bees to get in and out!" she called. "I've got the hose, but we've got to open one window part way and tape the hose in place!"

Let's see, Bob thought as he surveyed the swarming room. *It doesn't really matter which booth I take, as long as it's sort of near the door.* (That was in case he needed to whisk Ozzy outside for any reason.)

"Can you help me?" came a piercing little voice behind him.

Bob turned and saw the one kindergarten boy who'd decided to be in the science fair. He was clutching his balloon tightly and looking lost.

"Sure, I can help you," said Bob. "What's your name?"

"Peter."

"What do you need help with, Peter?"

"I need a booth for my 'speriment!" The little boy said plaintively.

"Hmm." Bob looked around. "Where is your experiment?"

"The *balloon*'s my 'speriment!' " Peter protested, yanking on the string. "I'm showing how if you draw a face on it and blow it up, the face gets bigger!"

Bob pursed his lips together thoughtfully, so that he wouldn't smile. "Sounds interesting," he said. "Well, then, how about if you take this booth right next to mine?"

Peter's face brightened. "Sure," he said happily. He taped the string of his balloon to the side of his booth. "Okay, see you tomorrow!" he said, and rushed out of the lunchroom.

"Can you give me a hand now, Bob?" It was Rocky. "I can't seem to find a booth that's big enough. They're all these little cheapo deals that real people can't fit into!"

Bob didn't answer him right away. He was trying to evaluate Rocky's stomach, which—now that he noticed it—suddenly seemed to be taking up an unfamiliar amount of space. "How's your project going?" he asked instead.

"Oh, fantastic," said Rocky. "It really worked! I've gained twenty-five pounds already!"

This time Bob couldn't help smiling. "Well, Rock, don't you think that may be why you can't find a booth that's wide enough?"

"Do you think so?" asked Rocky in amazement. "Maybe you're right! Hey, that will be a good thing to put into my description!"

Junior Smith rushed by them, his hands full of rolls of quarters.

"How's your project going, by the way?" said Rocky. "I haven't heard much about it."

"It's going fine," said Bob quickly.

Rocky was peering over his shoulder curiously. "Is that your booth? Where's all your stuff? Don't you have pictures or diagrams or something?"

"Oh, I can't bring my stuff until tomorrow," said Bob.

As long as I can get my stuff to walk here like a good ostrich.

"If we get caught," said Bonnie, "I am going to get in unbelievable amounts of trouble."

"Oh, come on," said Bob. "What kind of trouble? You're helping me with my science project!"

Bonnie gave him a withering glance. "Oh, that's right," she said. "I only snuck out of the house at eleven o'clock on a school night. We're only trespassing on the grounds of a country club. And we're only doing it to smuggle out a valuable ostrich that you're hiding from the zoo. I forgot—we couldn't possibly get into trouble over anything like that."

"Don't worry. No one's going to recognize you in that ostrich mask," said Bob gallantly. He shone his flashlight into the darkness ahead of him. "Here's the gully," he said. "Watch your step. Anyway, there's no other way to make sure Ozzy comes to school with us tomorrow. If he doesn't spend the night in my garage, how will I be sure he won't wander away tonight?"

"He never has before, has he?" asked Bonnie as she picked her way along the bank of the creek.

"Well, no," Bob admitted. "But that was before he was in love with you—with your mask, I mean. What if he decides to pick tonight to go looking for you?"

Since meeting Bonnie, Ozzy had become a changed bird. Every time Bob went to visit him, he found Ozzy pacing anxiously back and forth waiting for Bonnie to get there. If Bonnie hadn't come along, Ozzy would lie down on the ground and refuse to move.

Ozzy only loved Bonnie when she was wearing her mask, of course. The one time she'd gone to see him without it, he had turned and bolted halfway across the golf course. It wasn't exactly flattering.

Bonnie was wearing the mask that night, though. She looked a little creepy in the darkness, but Bob didn't tell her that. He was sure Ozzy wouldn't care.

And Ozzy didn't. He was sleeping in his nest when Bob and Bonnie reached him, but he sprang to his feet when Bonnie patted his head.

"Hi, Oz," said Bob softly. "Ready to take a trip?"

Ozzy didn't pay any attention. He was busy craning his head around to look into the painted eyes of Bonnie's mask.

"She's too sleepy to pay attention to you, Oz-boy," said Bob kindly. He slipped the leash around Ozzy's neck. "C'mon, buddy. Let's go. Bonnie, why don't you walk a little ahead of us? That way he'll be sure to go in the right direction. You can have the flashlight."

"Oh, all right," muttered Bonnie. "But I just want you to know that I'm only doing this for Ozzy. As far as *you're* concerned, I'm keeping score. You're going to have to pay me back for this in a big, big way."

Her ostrich head swaying back and forth, she led the way back to the street.

"Wait a minute!" Bob said suddenly. "I forgot your blankets!"

The blankets had been a last-minute inspiration of Bob's. He was hoping that if both Bonnie and Ozzy were draped in blankets, it would make Ozzy look more like a person in an ostrich costume. (Why two people would be wearing ostrich costumes was a question Bob hoped nobody would ask—or at least he hoped nobody would ask Ozzy.)

Bob slipped an army blanket over Ozzy's back and another over Bonnie's shoulders. Then he stepped back to see how they looked.

"Well," he said slowly, "it's not perfect. You look like someone in an ostrich costume, and he looks like an ostrich wearing a blanket. But maybe from far enough away, someone would think both of you were wearing costumes."

Ozzy walked quietly along next to Bob, his eyes fixed on Bonnie.

Maybe this won't be as hard as I thought, Bob said to himself. *It's going pretty smoothly now.*

But that was before he and Bonnie got Ozzy into the Kellys' garage.

The first thing Bonnie did was walk straight into the gas grill, stomach first.

"Oof!" she grunted.

With a dull clang, the grill tipped over onto the concrete floor.

Bob and Bonnie froze, but Ozzy didn't. The noise startled him so much that he jumped into the air and smashed into one of the garage walls.

There was a loud thud as Ozzy rebounded off the wall and fell to the floor. Only he didn't hit the floor. He hit the rowing machine. The seat slid forward and dumped him onto the ground.

"Ozzy!" Bob gasped. "Are you okay?" Quickly he knelt down beside Ozzy's still form. "Hand me the flashlight, Bon!"

"I can't find it!" wailed Bonnie in a whisper. "I dropped it when I banged into the grill!"

"Oh, no," said Bob. He was feeling around in the gloom to see if he could find Ozzy's pulse. But where *was* an ostrich's pulse? And even if he could find it, he had no idea what an ostrich's normal pulse would be.

Bonnie, meanwhile, was groping around on the floor for the flashlight. "Here it is!" she whispered, and thrust it into Bob's hand. "How is he?"

Bob shone the light into Ozzy's eyes. To his relief, the huge bird blinked protestingly and moved his head away from the beam. He wasn't unconscious after all.

"I think he's okay," said Bob. "But maybe we'd better get out of here before he stands up. Oh, no! Hurry, Bon! He *is* standing up!"

Quickly they darted out of the garage, and Bob yanked down the garage door.

"I bet he'll settle down once he's alone," he said without conviction. "Okay, Bon. Let's get you—uh-oh, here comes my father."

The noise from the garage had awakened him.

"Go around to the back!" Bob hissed at Bonnie. "I'll meet you later!"

Bonnie slipped around the side of the garage without a sound.

"H-hi, Dad," Bob quavered.

His father squinted sleepily at him from the back door. "Bob? What on earth are you doing out here?"

"I—I heard a noise from the garage!" said Bob. That was true, at least. "I came down to see what it was."

"Well? What was it?" asked his father.

"I don't know. I, uh, think I scared it away. But I closed the garage door just to make sure nothing comes back in."

"I bet it was that skunk of yours," his father said grumpily. "Oh, well. Let's go back to bed." When Bob didn't follow him in, his father turned around. "Well, what are you waiting for? Come on!"

So Bob had to go in with his father. Then he had to wait until his parents had fallen asleep to sneak out of the house and walk Bonnie home. What with one thing and another, he didn't get much sleep that night.

* * *

"What is that bumping sound outside?" asked Mrs. Kelly the next morning. She put down her coffee cup with a clatter.

"I bet it's a burglar!" shouted Lynn instantly. "Let me go out and zap him!"

Hand on holster, she jumped up and raced for the back door.

"Stop, Lynn!" croaked Bob. He was so tired his voice wasn't working right. "It's not a burglar! It's—it's just Bonnie and Diego changing into their costumes for the science fair!"

Thank heaven we thought of that line last night, he thought gratefully. *And thank heaven Bonnie didn't oversleep this morning. It was easy to let her into the garage before anyone else woke up.*

"What costumes?" asked Mrs. Kelly.

"Their ostrich costumes, of course!" said Bob. "Remember? I already told you about it!"

"What? When did you . . . I must have been distracted or something," said Bob's mother. "I don't remember you saying anything about costumes." She paused. "But why are they wearing *ostrich* costumes, though?" asked Mrs. Kelly confusedly.

"To be stupid," Lynn suggested.

"Mom!" said Bob impatiently. "I'm busy! I can't just keep telling you everything five million times!"

He pushed back his chair abruptly.

"I've got to go," he said. "They need me to help set things up at the lunchroom before school. Bye! Wish me luck!"

He dashed out the back door, raced over to the garage, and whipped open the garage door.

"Ready?" he asked.

"Let's get out of here! He's going crazy all cooped up like this," Bonnie said. She adjusted the blanket on Ozzy's back, straightened her mask, took a deep breath, and picked up her bike. Then she hopped on and pedaled down the driveway as hard as she could.

Ozzy pelted after her, with Bob holding tightly onto the leash. He had just a glimpse of his parents' startled faces through the kitchen window before the ostrich dragged him down the driveway.

As Mr. Haypence had reminded everyone, ostriches can run about forty miles an hour. Even though they weren't going nearly that fast, Bob's feet barely touched the ground as he strained to hold onto Ozzy's leash. They made it to school in six minutes.

Bonnie was just locking her bicycle into the bike rack as Ozzy and Bob came panting up. (Bob was panting, anyway.)

"Is it okay for me to take my mask off now?" she asked.

"Please, just wait until we're in the lunch-room," said Bob. "That way he'll follow you in without any trouble. As long as you don't mind, of course," he added.

"*I* don't," said Bonnie through clenched teeth, "as long as *you* don't mind owing me big-time for this, of course."

Then she looked at Ozzy, and her voice soft-ened. "I don't want you to get frightened, Oz," she cooed. "You follow me in and we'll do just fine."

They probably *would* have done just fine if Bonnie had been able to keep her ostrich mask on for the whole day. As she and Bob led Ozzy through the front door, he walked as quietly as a cat. He didn't even seem to notice the aston-ished people falling back as the little procession headed through the halls toward the lunchroom. He only looked around curiously, as if he were saying, "Hmm. Just another kind of zoo."

But when Bob and Bonnie led him into the lunchroom, everyone gathered in there started gasping and shrieking. And when Bonnie took off her mask and he realized that he was alone, Ozzy went crazy.

It was sheer bad luck that the booth he decided to knock down happened to be holding Bonnie and Tilly's beehive.

Chapter Nine
Ozzy the Champion!

Bob gave Ms. Wu and Mr. Haypence a shame-faced grin. "I'm sorry. I know I should have told you about it ahead of time, but—"

"You certainly should have!" said Mr. Haypence furiously. His lunchroom had been the scene of total bee-panic for the previous half-hour. Luckily (or unluckily, for him) Mr. Haypence had been the only person to be stung.

Well, it's your own fault you were stung, Bob wanted to tell him. Mr. Haypence had refused to listen when Bonnie had jumped up onto a booth and shouted, "Everyone freeze! The bees will calm down and go back into the hive if we don't bother them!" Everyone had frozen except Mr. Haypence. He had rushed toward the hive and tried to kick it out of the way. You couldn't blame the bees for getting mad about *that*.

But the bees were all safely back in the hive, and Ozzy had calmed down the instant he had spotted the balloon that belonged to Peter, the little boy whose booth was next to Bob's. (It must have reminded him of the zoo. He had stopped looking around for other ostriches and was staring blissfully at the balloon as it bobbed back and forth.) But Mr. Haypence wasn't back to normal yet—not even normal for *him*. He wanted to punish someone, and Bob was the most punishable person in the lunchroom at the moment.

"I'm waiting for you to explain this extraordinary occurrence, Mister Kelly," Mr. Haypence continued frostily.

"Well, I was working on my wildlife project, and then I found Ozzy. So I decided to have him be my project instead," Bob said.

"You mean you've known where this—this *creature* has been hiding all along?"

"For the past few weeks, anyway," Bob answered.

"So you've been hiding him from the zoo on *purpose*? That's criminal behavior!"

Just then Ms. Wu, who had been looking in the other direction, tapped the principal on the shoulder. "The other judges are here, Mr. Haypence," she said.

"Oh! Oh, my goodness, we'd better go and join them!" Mr. Haypence's bad mood vanished in an instant. He tugged on his tie, and he and Ms. Wu rushed off toward the little group of grown-ups that was coming through the lunchroom door.

Bob turned to Ozzy and leaned against his wing for a second. "I guess you're going to have to go back home today, buddy," he said sadly. "It's been fun, but there's no way I'm going to get to keep you."

But Bob had to admit that in some ways it would be a relief to have Ozzy go home, even if he did get in trouble with the zoo when he brought Ozzy back.

It's been hard having to keep such a big secret, he thought. *And it's been hard worrying that someone would find Ozzy, or that Ozzy would wander away into the street or something. I guess I don't like having that much responsibility. But I am still going to keep putting out food for the skunk and the other animals. At least until the golf course opens up again.*

Bob glanced over at Bonnie, who was smiling nervously as the judges walked over to her.

Besides, it was getting to the point where I couldn't handle Ozzy without Bonnie, he said to himself. *And somehow I don't think Bonnie really wanted to have to wear an ostrich mask for the rest of her life.*

He gave Ozzy a quick hug around the neck. "Be a good boy, Oz," he said, and tied Ozzy's leash around his chair. "I want to walk around and see some of the other projects."

"And did it work? Are you, uh, un-identical now?" one of the judges asked Larry Watson.

"Yes! Definitely!" he answered. "I mean, look at us!"

The judge, who was a high-school physics teacher, stared closely at the twins. "Actually, you still look pretty identical to me," she said. "Louie's face might be a little dirtier, but—"

"The dirt's not important!" exclaimed Larry. "We have *scientific results!* I'm a whole millimeter shorter than Louie now! And look—my nose is shorter than Louie's! That's un-identical, don't you think?"

"Most impressive!" Mr. Haypence exclaimed proudly.

The physics teacher didn't look quite as impressed. "Did you measure yourselves before you started the experiment?" she asked.

"Well, no, but—"

Bob wandered off before he could hear the rest of the answer. In a booth by the window, Jennifer was giving another judge a facial. "You have enormous pores," she was telling him importantly.

"I do? Gee, I didn't know that!" he answered.

"Well, I think we can make you look a lot better with some of my toning liquid."

"You can? How did you make that stuff, anyway?"

"Oh, it wasn't hard," said Jennifer. She was slapping the judge's cheeks vigorously. "It's got an alcohol base—alcohol's a great astringent—and then I put in a little propylene glycol to make it go on more smoothly."

Hey! She really knows what she's talking about! thought Bob in surprise. *She's not as big an airhead as I thought!*

Next to Jennifer, Bonnie and Tilly were chatting with Ms. Wu. "And what did you learn from this?" asked Ms. Wu.

"Well, the main thing we learned is that we're never going to eat honey again," said Bonnie.

Ms. Wu looked startled. "Why not?" she asked.

"Do you know how honey is made?" said Tilly.

"Sure! Bees make it out of nectar!"

"But do you know *how* they make it? I used to think they mixed it up with their legs or something, but they don't! They eat the nectar and then—uh, Bonnie, what's the scientific word?"

"Regurgitate," said Bonnie promptly.

"That's right!" said Tilly. "Honey is bee barf!"

Ms. Wu looked thoughtful. "That's interesting," she said slowly. "You know, I'm just starting to realize that I've never cared much for honey myself."

Bob stopped to see what was going on at Diego's booth, but he couldn't understand anything Diego and the judges were talking about. By the looks on their faces, neither could the judges.

But the judge at Rocky's table, a woman named Mrs. Bunsen, looked as if she understood all too well what Rocky was talking about.

"It's a great way to put on weight, too!" Rocky was saying. "You have to work up to it, though. It took me a while before I could drink heavy cream right out of the carton. But if you want some help, I'd be glad to work up a list of instructions for you."

"Thank you," said Mrs. Bunsen faintly.

"See, first you start by adding a little bit of butter to everything you—"

"Oops! I see that the other judges are calling me!" Mrs. Bunsen interrupted. "Thanks very much, Rocky!"

"I'm a shoo-in," Rocky told Bob proudly as they watched Mrs. Bunsen scurry away.

Unfortunately, he wasn't even a runner-up.

"Third prize goes to Jennifer Stevens," announced Ms. Wu ten minutes later.

Jennifer looked happier than Bob had ever seen her. "I won something?" she gasped. "I can't believe it!"

"You did a great job," Ms. Wu told her with a smile. She turned back out to her audience. "All of us were impressed by the tremendous amount of research Jennifer put into making her cosmetics, and her in-depth knowledge of the chemical properties of her ingredients."

I guess I'm glad I let her try out her makeup on me, Bob said to himself.

Ms. Wu was picking up the red ribbon now. "Second prize goes to Diego Lopez for his very sophisticated work in synthesizing glycoproteins."

There was a murmur of astonishment in the audience. "I can't believe he didn't win!" Bob heard someone say.

Diego looked a little surprised, too. But he was smiling as he bounded up to shake Ms. Wu's hand and get his ribbon.

"Too tough for you, huh?" he asked teasingly.

She nodded and smiled back at him. "For all of us. You probably would have won if you'd taken the time to explain your work more clearly," she said. "We were just bowled over by your results, but the steps leading up to them were too complicated to follow."

"I'll remember that next time," Diego promised.

Ms. Wu turned to the audience again.

"Now, it's not very often that we get the chance

to give the blue ribbon to the kind of project we're about to award it to," she said. "After all, it's very rare that we come into contact with a contestant who deals in wildlife on such a *large* scale."

Bob's heart started to pound.

I can't believe it! he thought.

"I'm talking about Bob Kelly, of course," said Ms. Wu.

The whole lunchroom burst into cheers. Ozzy flinched nervously, and Bob reached out to grab his leash.

"I knew he had done a first-rate job!" boomed Mr. Haypence. "That's just what I was telling him before the judges got here!"

Ms. Wu didn't even look at Mr. Haypence. "Bob, we don't completely approve of the fact that you concealed Ozzy from the zoo," she said. "But we're sure that even the zoo would agree that you did a great job taking care of him. He's obviously well-fed, and you took care of his emotional needs as well."

Bob grinned over at Bonnie. "That wasn't really me," he said.

"Well, you can share the ribbon with Bonnie if you want to," Ms. Wu told him. "In the meantime, why don't you come up and get it?"

"I'd be happy to," said Bob. "But could you just hold onto it for a few more minutes? Ozzy's yanking on the leash, and I think I'd better get him outside. Right now."

"What is *that*?" asked Bonnie.

"That," said Bob proudly, "is a baby shrew mole."

"A baby what?"

"Shrew mole. Isn't she cute?" Bob bent over the box he was holding and gave the tiny animal a pat. "Shrew moles are the smallest kind of North American mole," he said. "They eat earthworms and grubs and stuff like that."

"Where did you get it?" said Bonnie.

"You mean, where did I get *her*? The zoo gave her to me."

"They did? I was afraid they were going to arrest you!"

"Well, so was I," Bob confessed. "At least the people who came to pick Ozzy up at school seemed pretty mad at me. But then the director of the zoo called me the next day and asked me to come in and talk to him."

"Weren't you scared?"

"Of course! I was totally scared! But the director wasn't mad at all. He said Ozzy was in great shape, and that I can come and visit him whenever I want to."

"Can I, too?" asked Bonnie jealously. "After all, I'm really more his friend than you are!"

"Yes, you can. I even asked that. And he said that they didn't really feel as though they should give me a money reward for finding Ozzy, but was there some kind of animal I thought my parents would let me have? So we went to the animal nursery, and I picked out this shrew mole. I didn't see how my parents could possibly get upset about something so tiny."

"She's horribly ugly, though," said Bonnie, peering into the box. "The shrew mole, I mean. She just looks like a blob with a pointy nose."

"Bonnie, how can you say that? She's cute!" said Bob. "Anyway, Mom says I can keep her in my room as long as I never, never leave any earthworms lying around."

He gave the shrew mole a gentle nudge with his finger. An outsider might have said she didn't seem to notice, but Bob was sure she was looking lovingly up at him.

"Well, that's nice for you," said Bonnie. "A shrew mole and a blue ribbon. All *I* got out of the science fair was a broken beehive and an ostrich mask."

Bob looked up from the box. "You know, Bon, I wanted to say something about that. You really helped me a lot with Ozzy. I could never have taken care of him without you. And I just want you to know I haven't forgotten about it."

Bonnie's face brightened. "Thanks for noticing, anyway," she said.

"Oh, I did more than notice," Bob told her. "You remember how you said you hoped I'd pay you back some day for all your help? Well, I have."

"You have? What are you—"

With a wide smile, Bob pointed down at the shrew mole.

"I named her after you," he said.

**Meet the kids at Hollis Elementary
School. . . . They're smart and funny.
And their lunchroom is awesome. It's
where everything happens!**
by Ann Hodgman

___ #1: NIGHT OF A THOUSAND PIZZAS   0-425-12091-0/$2.75
___ #2: FROG PUNCH   0-425-12092-9/$2.75
___ #3: THE COOKIE CAPER   0-425-12132-1/$2.75
___ #4: THE FRENCH FRY ALIENS   0-425-12170-4/$2.75
___ #5: RUBBERBAND STEW   0-425-12267-0/$2.75
___ #6: THE FLYING POPCORN
        EXPERIMENT   0-425-12302-7/$2.75
___ #7: INVASION OF THE FAST FOOD   0-425-12349-9/$2.75
___ #8: SPACE FOOD   0-425-12441-X/$2.75
        (Coming in December)

For Visa and MasterCard orders call: 1-800-631-8571

FOR MAIL ORDERS: CHECK BOOK(S). FILL
OUT COUPON. SEND TO:

BERKLEY PUBLISHING GROUP
390 Murray Hill Pkwy., Dept. B
East Rutherford, NJ 07073

NAME_____

ADDRESS_____

CITY_____

STATE_____ ZIP_____

PLEASE ALLOW 6 WEEKS FOR DELIVERY.
PRICES ARE SUBJECT TO CHANGE WITHOUT NOTICE.

POSTAGE AND HANDLING:
$1.00 for one book, 25¢ for each ad-
ditional. Do not exceed $3.50.

BOOK TOTAL $ _____

POSTAGE & HANDLING $ _____

APPLICABLE SALES TAX $ _____
(CA, NJ, NY, PA)

TOTAL AMOUNT DUE $ _____

PAYABLE IN US FUNDS.
(No cash orders accepted.)   295a

WHEN TWO FAMILIES GET TOGETHER UNDER THE SAME ROOF, IT'S...

SCRAMBLED EGGS

BY SUZANNE ALLEN

Seven kids, five cats, two turtles, and one very big dog take up a lot of space!

___#1: SUDDENLY SISTERS 0-425-12217-4/$2.75
When Berry Sterling's mother marries Terri Turner's father, their new family is too big! Berry and Terri are both nine, but no way are Miss Messy and Miss Prissy like twins. Each girl has a secret plan to get her own room. Will the plans work, or will Berry and Terri drive each other crazy first?

___#2: ALMOST STARRING DAD 0-425-12218-2/$2.75
When Berry and Terri enter a video contest, Dad is in for a major surprise, because he's going to be the star! Making a video is hard work, especially when it's a secret. And when Dad finds out who the video is for, he's going to hit the roof!

For Visa and MasterCard orders call: 1-800-631-8571

FOR MAIL ORDERS: CHECK BOOK(S). FILL OUT COUPON. SEND TO:

BERKLEY PUBLISHING GROUP
390 Murray Hill Pkwy., Dept. B
East Rutherford, NJ 07073

NAME_____

ADDRESS _____

CITY_____

STATE _____ ZIP _____

PLEASE ALLOW 6 WEEKS FOR DELIVERY.
PRICES ARE SUBJECT TO CHANGE WITHOUT NOTICE.

POSTAGE AND HANDLING:
$1.00 for one book, 25¢ for each additional. Do not exceed $3.50.

BOOK TOTAL	$ ____
POSTAGE & HANDLING	$ ____
APPLICABLE SALES TAX (CA, NJ, NY, PA)	$ ____
TOTAL AMOUNT DUE	$ ____

PAYABLE IN US FUNDS.
(No cash orders accepted.)

298